The Golly Sisters Go West

The Golly Sisters Go West

by
Betsy Byars

pictures by
Sue Truesdell

HarperTrophy
A Division of HarperCollins*Publishers*

I Can Read Book is a registered trademark of
HarperCollins Publishers.

The Golly Sisters Go West
Text copyright © 1985 by Betsy Byars
Illustrations copyright © 1985 by Susan G. Truesdell

Designed by Trish Parcell

Library of Congress Cataloging-in-Publication Data
Byars, Betsy Cromer.
  The Golly Sisters go West.

  (An I can read book)
  Summary: May-May and Rose, the singing, dancing Golly
sisters, have several adventures while traveling west by
covered wagon, entertaining people along the way.
  1. Children's stories, American. [1. Entertainers—
Fiction. 2. Frontier and pioneer life—Fiction. 3. West
(U.S.)—Fiction] I. Truesdell, Sue, ill. II. Title.
III. Series.
PZ7.B9836Gol 1986   [E]   84-48474
ISBN 0-06-020883-X
ISBN 0-06-020884-8 (lib. bdg.)
ISBN 0-06-444132-6 (pbk.)

First Harper Trophy edition, 1989.

For Paul and Scott

Table of Contents

The Golly Sisters Go West

The Golly sisters sat in their wagon.

They were going west.

"Go," May-May said to the horse.

The horse did not go.

"This makes me mad," May-May said.

"Our wagon is ready.

Our songs and dances are ready.

And the horse will not go."

"It makes me mad too," said Rose.

"Something is wrong with this horse."

Rose got down from the wagon.

May-May got down too.

They walked around the horse.

"Do you see anything wrong?"

May-May asked.

"No, but something is wrong,"
said Rose.

"When we say, 'Go,'
the horse does not go."

"And if the horse does not go,
we do not go," said May-May.

Suddenly, Rose said,

"Sister!

I just remembered something.

There is a horse word for 'go.'"

"A horse word?" said May-May.

"What is it?"

"Giddy-up!" Rose said.

The horse went.

"Stop! Stop!" cried May-May.

"Is there a horse word for stop?"

"Whoa," said Rose.

"WHOA!" cried May-May.

The horse stopped.

The sisters got into the wagon.

Rose took the reins.

"Giddy-up, horse," she said.

The horse went.

May-May said,

"Now that we know the right words,

we can go west."

"Yes," said Rose.

"We are on our way!"

The Golly Sisters Give a Show

It was the Golly sisters' first show.

They peeped around the curtain.

Men and women were there.

Children were there.

Even dogs were there.

"Oh, am I ready!" said May-May.

"You open the curtain,

and I will go first."

SHOW
TODAY

"I want to go first," said Rose.

"You got to wear the blue dress,

so I get to go first," said May-May.

20

"I got to wear the blue dress because you look funny in blue," said Rose.

"Who says I look funny in blue?" asked May-May.

"Everybody!" said Rose.

"Give me the name of one person
who says I look funny in blue."

"Everybody!" said Rose.

"I knew it," said May-May.

"You cannot think of one person."

"I can."

"Cannot!"

"Can!"

"Then who?"

"Hmmmm, let me think," said Rose.

"See! There is not one person.

Admit it! Admit it! Admit it!"

cried May-May.

"All right, I admit it," said Rose.

"We will both go first.

We will sing and dance together."

Rose pulled the curtain.

"Oh, dear," May-May said,

"everyone got tired and went home.

Are you going to cry, Rose?"

"No," said Rose.

"Everyone did not go home.

The dogs are still here."

"Sister, do we give shows for dogs?"

"I do," said Rose.

"Then I do too," said May-May.

So May-May and Rose

gave a show for the dogs.

"This is wonderful!" May-May said.

"It sure is," sang Rose.

The Golly Sisters Get Lost

"We are lost," May-May said.

"I was afraid of that," said Rose.

"Are you worried, May-May?"

"No. I know what to do

when I am lost."

"You do? What?" asked Rose.

"First," said May-May,

"get in the back of the wagon.

Second,

make a cup of tea.

Third—"

"Wait, May-May, let me stop the horse.

I cannot make tea when he is moving."

28

"No!" said May-May.

"Do *not* stop the horse.

That is the *third* thing."

"Is there a fourth thing?" asked Rose.

"Yes!" said May-May. "Sing!

You start, Rose."

"Okay,"

said Rose.

"I will sing

'The Lost Gollys.'

It is about us."

Rose sang.

"Now it is my turn,"

said May-May.

"I will sing

'The Brave Gollys.'

It is about us too."

30

While May-May sang,

the wagon kept moving.

Then Rose sang again,

then May-May sang.

Then they sang together.

"I wonder if we are still lost?"
asked May-May.

"I will check," said Rose.

Just then they heard clapping.

They looked out of the wagon.

They were in the middle of a town.

Men and women were there.

Children and dogs were there.

34

"We gave a show!" May-May said.

"A wonderful show!" said Rose.

"We should get lost more often!"

35

The Golly sisters bowed.

"Thank you, thank you," they said.

36

The Horse Gives a Show

"I want the horse to dance
in the show," said May-May.
"No, May-May," said Rose,
"the horse cannot dance."

37

"Give him a chance, Rose.

Remember when we started?

No one thought *we* could dance.

No one thought we could sing."

"May-May, the horse cannot dance!"

"Trust me, Rose. You say—
*Here is my sister, May-May,
and her dancing horse,* and
the horse and I will do the rest."

That night May-May got on the horse.

"We are ready," she called.

Rose said to the people,

"Here is my sister, May-May,

and her dancing horse."

"Let's go, horse,"

May-May said.

The horse

did not move.

"Here is my sister,

May-May,

and her dancing horse,"

Rose said again.

"Come on, horse,"

said May-May.

The horse did not move.

Rose said, "While we are waiting

for May-May and her dancing horse,

I will sing a song."

When May-May heard that,

she said, "Giddy-up!"

The horse moved!

He jumped onto the stage.

He jumped off the stage.

May-May screamed, *"Eeeeeeeeee!"*

The horse ran through the town.

The horse ran out of the town.

"Well, that is too bad," Rose said.

"There will be no dancing horse.

No May-May either.

But do not worry.

I will do her songs and dances."

Late that night, May-May came back.

She fell onto her bed.

"Sister, you were right," she said.

"The horse cannot dance."

"May-May, are you ready?" asked Rose.

"No, I am not!" said May-May.

"My song is 'In My Pretty Red Hat,'

and I cannot find my red hat!"

"Want me to go first?" asked Rose.

"All right, but this makes me mad.

It was *my* turn to go first."

While Rose was singing,

May-May looked for her hat.

When Rose came off the stage,

May-May was still looking

for her hat.

"I want my hat!" she yelled.

"Did you
look under
my bed?"
asked Rose.

"Why would my hat

be under your bed?"

May-May asked.

She looked under Rose's bed.

There was the hat!

50

"Now I am really mad," said May-May.

"You *hid* my hat!"

"No harm has been done, May-May.

You can sing now," said Rose.

"I wanted to sing first!

First! First! First!"

yelled May-May.

"Stop!" cried Rose.

"You are squashing my hair.

May-May! Stop!"

May-May stopped

and looked at her hat.

"Rose!" she said.

"First I could not sing

because I could not find my hat.

Now I cannot sing

because I squashed my hat."

"My hair, too," said Rose.

"Rose," said May-May,

"tell the people

I will do a sad dance,

'The Dance of the Squashed Hat.'"

"People," said Rose, "here is May-May

and 'The Dance of the Squashed Hat.'"

May-May danced.

The people began to clap.

May-May turned to her sister.

"I forgive you, Rose," she said.

"I forgive you too," said Rose.

The Golly Sisters Are Scared

It was a dark night.

There was no moon.

"I hear something," May-May said.

"Something is outside our wagon."

"What will we do?" asked Rose.

"One of us will have to go outside,"

said May-May.

"I heard the noise, so you go."

"Why should *I* go?

It's your noise," said Rose.

"Do I have to do everything?"

asked May-May.

"I am not going to go," said Rose.

"Then I'm not going to go either,"
said May-May. "Nyah!"

"Nyah yourself!" said Rose.

May-May sat up.

"Remember our first show, Rose? Remember how we fussed because you said I look funny in blue?"

"Yes, I remember," said Rose.

"I remember we fussed so long that everyone went home."

60

"Maybe we have done it again,"

May-May said.

"I do not hear anything now, do you?"

"I do not hear a thing," said Rose.

May-May said, "Rose,

we must never fuss again,

unless..."

"Unless we hear something outside our wagon," Rose said.

"Rose,

that is what *I* was going to say.

You did not let me finish!

Why did you say—"

"May-May?"

"What?"

"Good night."

"Good night, Rose."

And the moon came out.

And the stars shone.

And the Golly sisters fell asleep.